This book belongs to:

....

To my girls, who can be dragon dancers too.
Joyce

To my inspiring parents, with love.
Jérémy

American edition published in 2018 by Lantana Publishing Ltd., London, UK.
www.lantanapublishing.com

First published in the United Kingdom in 2015 by Lantana Publishing Ltd.
info@lantanapublishing.com

Text © Joyce Chng 2018
Illustration © Jérémy Pailler 2018

Distributed in the United States and Canada by Lerner Publishing Group, Inc.
241 First Avenue North, Minneapolis, MN 55401 U.S.A.

For reading levels and more information, look for this title at
www.lernerbooks.com.

Printed and bound in Hong Kong.
Cataloging-in-Publication Data Available.

ISBN: 978-1-911373-26-1
eBook ISBN: 978-1-911373-30-8

Dragon Dancer

Joyce CHNG . Jérémy PAILLER

LANTANA
PUBLISHING

*I*t was the eve of the Lunar New Year. Yao, the dragon dancer, entered the room where Shen Long rested.

Shen Long was an ancient dragon. His great amber eyes were like full moons and his scales glittered like silver-blue sequins.

So, little one, have you come to wake me?

Yao knew that the voice of the dragon wasn't real. But to him it sounded like the gentle hiss of dry brown leaves, the shimmer of heat on a blue sky day.

Yao had heard Shen Long speak ever since he was a little boy.

"Yes, Shen Long," Yao replied, a little afraid and a little excited.

Then what are you waiting for, little one?

Shen Long's answer was almost a growl. His sky blue voice became a murky rain storm.

Yao's hands reached up and pulled away the protective plastic cover, peeling it off carefully.

There was a rumble, as if from the bones of the earth, as Shen Long's body unfolded inch by inch.

Are you ready to dance?

The voice was amused now, scornful and proud. Yao clenched his fists, angry at the dragon's tone.

"Yes." Another deep breath. "Yes, I am."

BOOM!
BOOM!
BOOM!

The next day, drum beats echoed off the walls, throbbing through the shopping mall like an earthquake.

Shen Long slid into the modern foyer in a silver-blue wave, dancing to the drums and the cymbals. A crowd had gathered to watch the dance, children covering their ears at the din.

Yao gripped the pole, his palms sweating. *Long tou. Dragon head.* Shen Long's power tugged at him like leashed lightning. Yao wished his grandpa had been there to see him.

DANCE, DANCE, DANCE!

Shen Long's voice was the sound of a thunderstorm. He circled the foyer of the shopping mall, claiming his territory, sniffing out the bad luck like a hunting hound.

Yao could sense dark pools of stale luck, like sticky black goo, bringing misfortune to everyone who had gathered there.

It was time to dance.

Suddenly Shen Long shot up into the air, taking Yao
with him. The two of them – dragon and boy – began
to loop and dip, cork-screwing through the shopping
mall to draw out the bad luck.

Streams of blackness, invisible
to the crowd, streaked towards
them. Yao and Shen Long
spiralled skywards, spinning the
blackness into a tight ball.

So much bad luck, Shen Long growled,
his voice like a small-scale hail storm.

They danced around the black ball
like a big cat playing with a toy.

BOOM! BOOM! BOOM!

Shen Long hissed, his scales flashing.
Cymbals clashed, bringing the sound of war.

NOW, NOW, NOW!

Dragon and boy drew down the colors
of the sun, mixing them into the ball.

Something was happening now: the black crackling, warring with the bright gold. As Yao and Shen Long danced, the black disappeared, replaced by the solar gold.

Laughing with triumph, dragon and boy chased the golden ball around.

People clapped and children cheered, but Yao did not hear it. All he knew was the rustling of spring rain and the rumbling of rolling thunder clouds, and the triumph of having chased the bad luck away.

He was a proper dragon dancer now!

With a shout, Yao and Shen Long sent the good luck spiraling back into the shopping mall where it belonged.

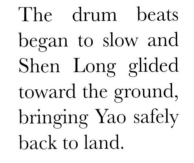

The drum beats began to slow and Shen Long glided toward the ground, bringing Yao safely back to land.

There was joy in the dragon's body as Yao steered him outside.

Yao hoped he had done his grandpa proud.

That night, Shen Long curled up with his eyes shining like moons. Yao would always remember those eyes. He had watched his grandpa bring Shen Long to life by dotting his eyes with black ink. From that day onwards, Shen Long had become a *tian long*, a sky dragon.

You are a good dragon dancer, Shen Long said, settling down to rest.

Yao grinned. Shen Long had never praised him before.

Shen Long's voice faded
into a murmuring of rain
clouds. He would sleep,
until Yao roused him for
the next dance.

Chinese New Year

Chinese New Year is celebrated across the globe. Festivities last for two weeks, culminating in *Yuan Xiao*, the Lantern Festival. It is a time not only to welcome spring after the harshness of winter, but also a time for family reunion.

As a child, I received many red packets containing money from my grandparents, parents and relatives. I also enjoyed yummy delicacies and wore new clothes, new shoes and new pajamas, because it is traditional to wear new things to welcome in the new year. We would give the house a thorough spring-clean and remove any junk, unused items or old appliances. These would be thrown away or given to charity. By accumulating too many old things, you retain too much yin energy, which is bad luck, so removing these old things invites good luck and prosperity.

Lion and dragon dance troops dance in shopping malls, homes and restaurants so that these places can enjoy good luck and prosperity for the rest of the year. This tradition inspired *Dragon Dancer*, in which Shen Long and Yao dance the bad luck away and invite the good luck in. The loud drum beats, cymbals and fire crackers accompanying lion and dragon dances remind us of how these New Year celebrations first began. It is said that Nian, a monstrous creature, was once rampaging through a village in search of food. It was only when the villagers began making loud noises and bangs that Nian was finally frightened away.

Can you spot Shen Long protecting Yao even while the dragon sleeps?

Joyce Chng